The Snowman

Raymond Briggs

PUFFIN

Other books
by Raymond Briggs

FATHER CHRISTMAS
FATHER CHRISTMAS GOES ON HOLIDAY
JIM AND THE BEANSTALK
FUNGUS THE BOGEYMAN

Based on Raymond Briggs' original story

THE SNOWMAN AND THE SNOWDOG BOOK AND CD

PUFFIN BOOKS

UK | USA | Canada | Ireland | Australia | India | New Zealand | South Africa

Puffin Books is part of the Penguin Random House group of companies
whose addresses can be found at global.penguinrandomhouse.com.

www.penguin.co.uk   www.puffin.co.uk   www.ladybird.co.uk

Penguin
Random House
UK

First published by Hamish Hamilton 1978
Published by Puffin Books 1980
Published in this edition 2014
004

Printed in China
A CIP catalogue record for this book is available from the British Library

ISBN: 978–0–723–29742–0

All correspondence to:
Puffin Books, Penguin Random House Children's
80 Strand, London WC2R 0RL

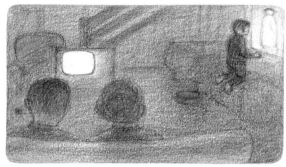

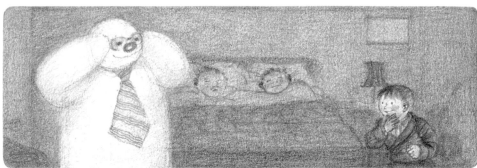

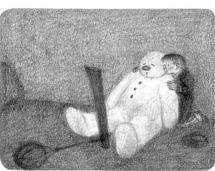

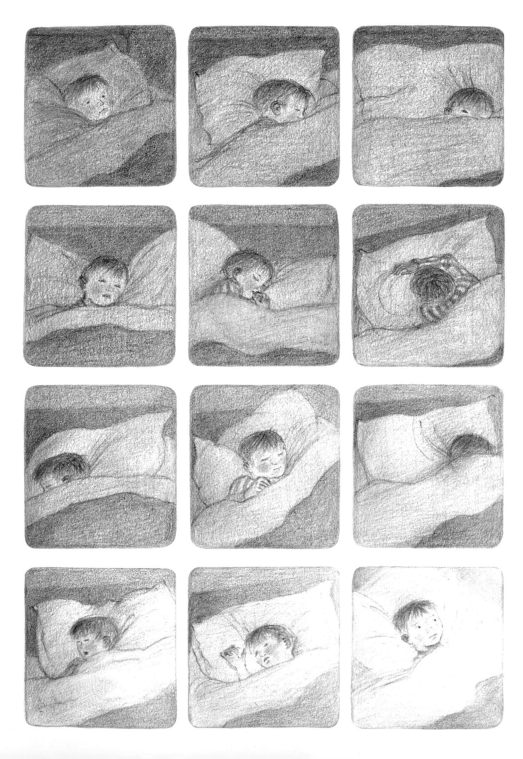